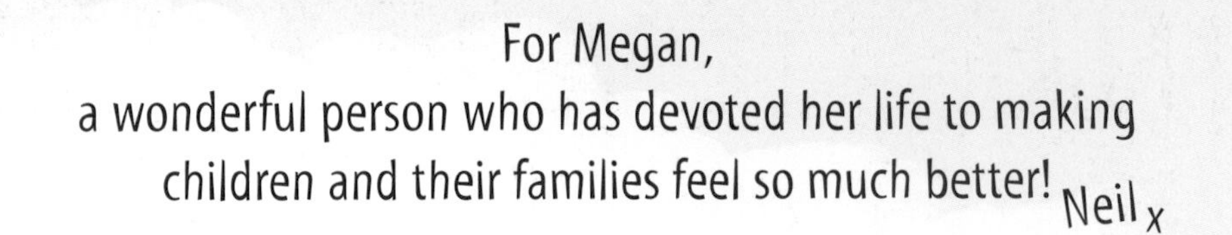

For Megan,
a wonderful person who has devoted her life to making
children and their families feel so much better! Neil x

For Isaac, Elliot and Maddison.
Auntie Janette x

Red Robin Books is an imprint of Corner To Learn Limited

Published by
Corner To Learn Limited
Willow Cottage • 26 Purton Stoke
Swindon • Wiltshire SN5 4JF • UK
www.redrobinbooks.com

ISBN: 978-1-905434-17-6

First published in the UK 2008

Design by
David Rose

Printed and bound by
Times Offset, Malaysia

Where have you two been?
Neil Griffiths
Illustrated by Janette Louden

"Race you home!" called Prickle.
"You don't stand a chance,"
boasted Antlery.

“Bet I’ll beat you!”
said Prickle hopefully.
“Bet you won’t,”
replied Antlery confidently.

"Right, we'll see...
on your marks...
get set... go!"

Antlery leapt into the lead and galloped off through the clearing. Prickle trotted behind him as fast as his little legs would carry him.

Antlery headed on
across the meadow and
dashed out of sight.

Prickle struggled
his way through
the long grass.

Antlery took the shortest route under the low branches of the horse chestnut tree. But this was his undoing as his antlers got thoroughly tangled!

Prickle's tiny feet crunched their way over the woodland floor.

Once untangled, Antlery bounded over a garden hedge and lost his way in a long line of washing.

Prickle scampered through a hole in the hedge and daintily tiptoed through the flowerbeds.

Antlery ran round and round in
circles until he could finally see
again and headed for the gateway.

Prickle dodged Antlery's hooves and headed for the gateway too.

Antlery sped down the
hill towards home.

Prickle took a deep breath, curled up tightly into a ball and began to roll faster and faster until he eventually overtook Antlery.

Antlery was beginning
to slow down, worn out by the
weight on his antlers. Then Prickle
began to slow down too as he caught more
and more leaves on his spines.

But neither could
stop until…

. . . bang!

They both collided
into the old oak tree.

"And where have you two been?"
asked two startled mothers.
"Nowhere!" came the reply
from the dazed pair.

But I'm not sure
their mothers quite
believed them.
Do you?

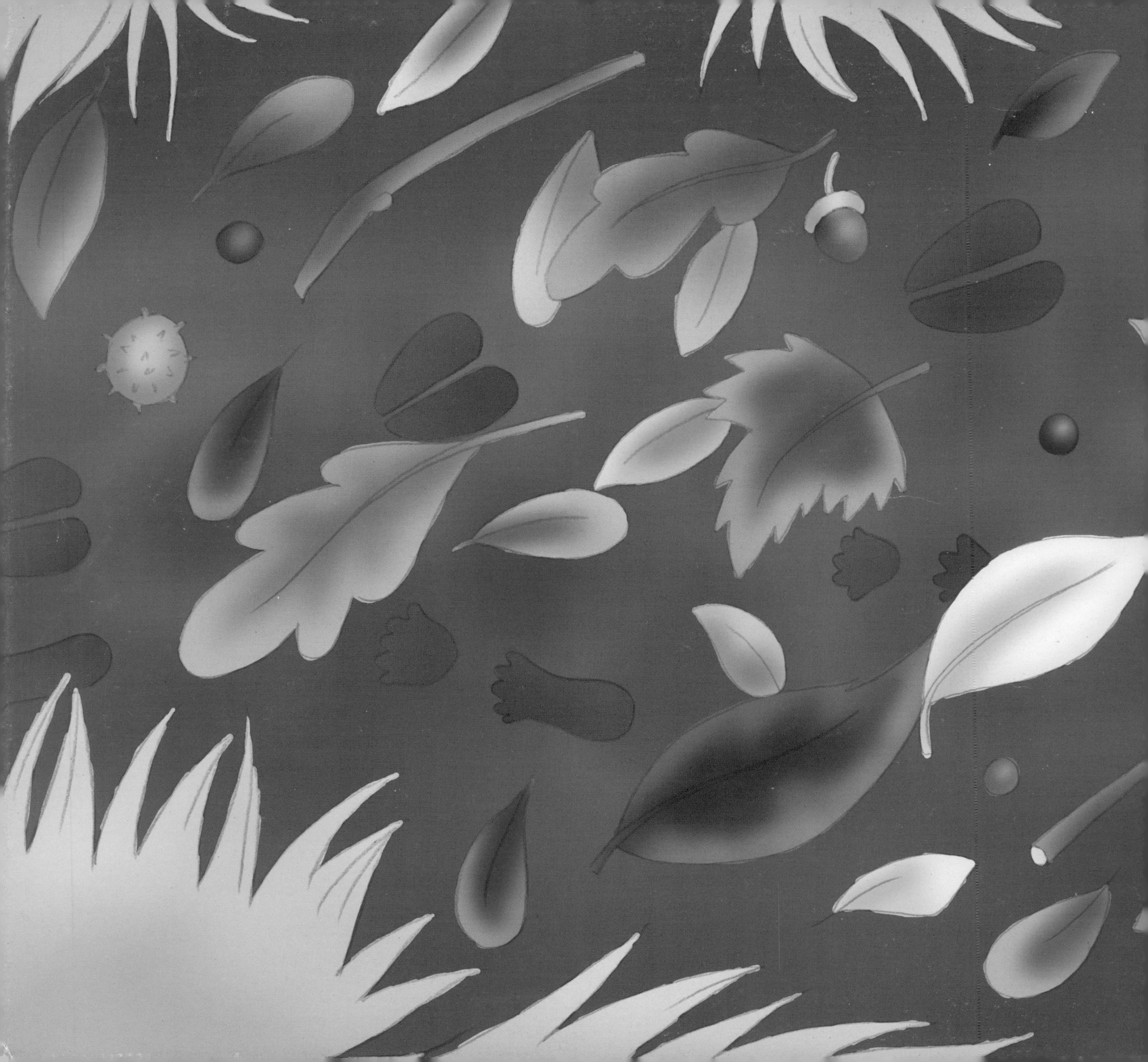